W9-ARO-053

Where will they go next?

The postcard predicts
an eerie expedition!

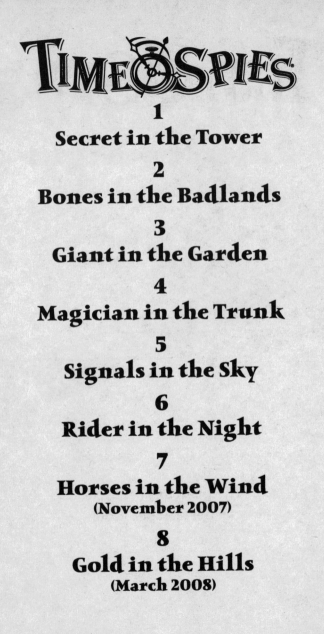

TIME SPIES

Time Spies
Rider in the Night
A Tale of Sleepy Hollow

By Candice Ransom
Illustrated by Greg Call

MIRRORSTONE

RIDER IN THE NIGHT

All characters, with the exception of the actual historical figures portrayed in this book, are fictitious and any resemblance to actual persons, living or dead, is purely coincidental.

This book is protected under the copyright laws of the United States of America. Any reproduction or unauthorized use of the material or artwork contained herein is prohibited without the express written permission of Wizards of the Coast, Inc.

Published by Wizards of the Coast, Inc. TIME SPIES, MIRRORSTONE and their respective logos are trademarks of Wizards of the Coast, Inc., in the U.S.A. and other countries.

All Wizards of the Coast characters, character names, and the distinctive likenesses thereof are property of Wizards of the Coast, Inc.

Printed in the U.S.A.

The sale of this book without its cover has not been authorized by the publisher. If you purchased this book without a cover, you should be aware that neither the author nor the publisher has received payment for this stripped book.

Cover and Interior art by Greg Call
First Printing: September 2007

9 8 7 6 5 4 3 2 1

ISBN: 978-0-7869-4354-8
620-10988740-001-EN

Library of Congress Cataloging-in-Publication Data

Ransom, Candice F., 1952-
Rider in the night / Candice Ransom ; illustrated by Greg Call.
p. cm. — (Time spies ; 6)
"Mirrorstone."
Summary: The time travel missions continue for Mattie, her brother Alex, and sister Sophie when they meet the superstitious residents in Washington Irving's classic story "The Legend of Sleepy Hollow," and must help fearful Ichabod Crane win the heart of Katrina Van Tassel.
  ISBN 978-0-7869-4354-8
[1. Time travel—Fiction. 2. Magic—Fiction. 3. Characters in literature—Fiction. 4. Superstition—Fiction. 5. Brothers and sisters—Fiction.] I. Call, Greg, ill. II. Title.
PZ7.R176Ri 2007
[Fic]—dc22   3/08 Fic Ran

                                                                          2007008814

U.S., CANADA,   EUROPEAN HEADQUARTERS
ASIA, PACIFIC, & LATIN AMERICA   Hasbro UK Ltd
Wizards of the Coast, Inc.   Caswell Way
P.O. Box 707   Newport, Gwent NP9 0YH
Renton, WA 98057-0707   GREAT BRITAIN
+1-800-324-6496   Please keep this address for your records

Visit our Web site at www.mirrorstonebooks.com

To Sherri

Contents

Halloween in July

"I bet that's her!" Mattie Chapman watched a strawberry-red truck roll up the dusty driveway. "Maybe this Travel Guide will send us someplace cooler."

"Yeah," said her brother Alex. "Like the North Pole."

"Ellsworth likes hot weather." Sophie, who was five, walked her stuffed elephant along the porch railing.

They were sitting on the front steps of the Gray Horse Inn. Although the sun was setting over Wildcat Mountain, it was still hot outside. The thermometer nailed to the porch post read ninety-six degrees.

The truck crunched to a stop in the gravel parking space. A woman wearing a white cotton sundress and sandals climbed out.

"Hello," she said to the kids. "Hot enough for you?"

Mattie jumped off the steps. "Hi! I'm Mattie Chapman. This is my brother Alex and this is Sophie. We'll take your stuff up to your room."

To the magical Jefferson Suite! she thought excitedly.

"I'm Mrs. Sullivan," the woman replied. "I only have one bag."

"I'll get it." Alex reached into the back of the pickup and lifted a small suitcase. "This is like a feather. Some of our guests must fill their suitcases with rocks!"

"I believe in traveling light." The woman reached into the cab for her purse.

Mattie whispered to Alex, "I wonder if she travels *light* as in *disappear*?"

The Travel Guides never stayed more than one night. And no one ever saw them check out the next morning. Mattie had never been able to figure out that mystery.

"What a beautiful house!" said Mrs. Sullivan.

Mattie raced up the path to the porch. When her family had moved from Maryland to an old house in Virginia earlier that summer, Mattie thought, *No way*. She knew she wouldn't like living in the country.

Her parents had turned the old house into a bed and breakfast. Guests stayed overnight and ate breakfast with them.

But *some* guests were extra-special. People who booked the Jefferson Suite sent the kids on incredible adventures. Now a new Travel Guide had arrived. And tomorrow morning, the kids would be off on a new mission!

Mattie ran into the house. "Mrs. Sullivan's here!"

Her mother came down the hall, smiling at the guest. "Hello, I'm Elise Chapman. Would you like a cold drink?"

"Sounds heavenly," Mrs. Sullivan replied.

"I'll just be a minute," said Mrs. Chapman, leaving for the kitchen.

Sophie led the way into the Keeping Room. "Guess what Mommy and I did today?" she asked Mrs. Sullivan. "We went through some boxes and I found—"

"Sophie." Mattie put her index finger to her lips.

They were supposed to be friendly to guests, but not pester them. Anyway, Mattie wanted to ask the Travel Guide some questions.

"I suppose you'll be going to Monticello tomorrow," Mattie said. So far all the Travel Guides had gone to Thomas Jefferson's home to give a lecture or see something.

Mrs. Sullivan settled in a chair. "No, I won't."

"You won't?" Alex said.

"I've already *been* to Monticello."

Mattie stared at Alex. What did this mean? The Travel Guides always did things exactly the same way. First they spent the night in the third-floor room. The next day each Travel Guide wrote a postcard, giving a hint about the mission, and then he or she left for Monticello.

"What did you do there?" asked Mattie.

5

"I looked for Thomas Jefferson's ghost," said Mrs. Sullivan.

Alex's jaw dropped. "Wow! Did you see it?"

"No, and I didn't hear it either," she said. "Let me explain. I'm a folklorist—I study the traditions, sayings, and stories of American people. My specialty is ghost stories. I travel all over the country, collecting ghost stories. Sometimes I visit places that are supposed to be haunted."

"Is Monticello haunted?" Mattie asked.

"For years tour guides and other people who work there have reported hearing someone humming in the gardens," said Mrs. Sullivan. "It always happens after the mansion is closed, so it can't be a tourist."

"Then who is doing the humming?" asked Alex.

Mrs. Sullivan shook her head. "That's just it. No one knows. Some people think it's

Thomas Jefferson. He used to hum when he worked in his garden."

Mattie tried to picture the third president pulling weeds and humming. "Alex thinks our house might be haunted. One time we heard a scratching sound in the attic."

"*You* heard it," said Alex. "When we went up there, we didn't hear it."

Mattie frowned at him. "It doesn't matter. I don't believe in ghosts anyway." She turned to Mrs. Sullivan. "Do you ever get scared?"

"Once in a while," Mrs. Sullivan said.

Mattie nodded. She was nine, a whole year older than Alex. But a couple of times she had become frightened on their adventures.

"I don't just hunt ghosts," Mrs. Sullivan said. "I'm also a storyteller. Mostly I tell ghost stories. Halloween is my favorite holiday!"

"Mine too!" Alex said. "I love Halloween parties."

"I wish it were Halloween now," Mattie said, pushing her bangs off her forehead.

"October *would* feel good right about now," said Mrs. Chapman, coming in with a pitcher of lemonade and glasses. "This must be the hottest July on record. It was too hot to bake shortbread. I thought we'd have fruit instead."

Mr. Chapman followed, carrying a tray with a bowl of strawberries and a large round watermelon. "I'll cut the melon," he said. "Who wants the first slice?"

"I have an idea," Mattie said. "Let's have a Halloween in July party! We can bob for apples and eat doughnuts—"

"We don't have any doughnuts," Mrs. Chapman said. "Or apples."

"We don't have a pumpkin either," Sophie pointed out. "For a jack-o'-lantern."

Alex thumped the watermelon. "We'll carve a melon-o'-lantern!"

"Can we, Daddy?" Mattie asked.

"I'll get some newspapers," he answered. "Be very careful with the knife."

After newspapers were spread on the coffee table, Alex cut the top off the watermelon. Then Mattie scooped out pink chunks into a bowl. She and Alex argued over what kind of face to carve.

"I'll do the eyes and nose," Mattie said. "And you do the mouth."

"What about me?" Sophie asked.

"Soph, you're too little to use the knife," said Mr. Chapman.

As Mattie carefully cut a jagged nose in the rind, she noticed Sophie leave the room. She hoped her little sister wasn't upset.

"Ta da!" Alex exclaimed, waving his hand over the completed melon-o'-lantern. "All we need is a candle and the Halloween in July party will officially begin."

The melon-o'-lantern leaked onto the platter.

"It's kind of mushy," Mattie said.

Mrs. Chapman looked dubiously at the squishy melon-o'-lantern. "How about if I light candles instead?" She lit the candles on the mantel.

"And how about if I tell my favorite ghost story?" Mrs. Sullivan offered.

"Cool!" said Mattie and Alex together.

"Wait for me!"

A small figure burst into the room wearing a green satin dress and a purple satin cape decorated with stars and moons.

"Sophie!" Mattie exclaimed. "That's my old Halloween costume. Where did you find it?"

"I told you—Mommy and me were unpacking boxes today." Sophie held up her stuffed elephant. "Look! I made a cape for Ellsworth too."

Mattie touched the black and orange design on the bottom of Sophie's skirt. "I loved this costume. I wore it all the time, even to bed."

"I'm going to wear this dress to bed too," Sophie declared.

"Sophie, you are a wonderful witch,"

said Mrs. Sullivan. She patted the seat beside her. "Will you sit with me while I tell my story?"

Sophie climbed into the chair and cuddled Ellsworth in the crook of her arm.

Mattie and Alex sat on the braided rug. Mr. Chapman switched off the lamp. The candles' flames sketched spooky shadows on the wall.

Mrs. Sullivan's voice was low. "Gather 'round, listeners, and I'll tell you an old story."

Mattie settled into a comfortable position.

"Once," Mrs. Sullivan began, "there was a village nestled in the Catskill Mountains along the Hudson River in New York State. The village was called Sleepy Hollow. Everything about Sleepy Hollow was sleepy. The brook moved drowsily between its banks. The people walked around as if they were in a dream."

She paused.

"But even though it was a peaceful place, Sleepy Hollow was *haunted*. The woods were haunted. The brook was haunted. The bridge over the brook was haunted. Ghosts and goblins lurked everywhere."

Mattie felt the back of her neck prickle.

"The villagers"—Mrs. Sullivan went on, dropping her voice to a whisper—"never knew when a ghost or a goblin would fly at them—"

Out of nowhere, something black and hairy leaped across the room and landed in the middle of Mattie's lap.

She screamed!

— 2 —

The Ghost of Gray Horse Inn

"Winchester!" Mattie shoved the big black cat off her lap.

Alex hooted with laughter. "You thought Winchester was a ghost!"

"I did not," said Mattie hotly. "I don't believe in ghosts."

"Maybe you will after this story," said Mrs. Sullivan. She cleared her throat and continued.

"One man in Sleepy Hollow was *really* afraid of the supernatural. He was the village schoolteacher, and his name was Ichabod Crane. He wasn't much to look at—tall, thin, and gawky. One day, Ichabod saw the richest man in the village, Baltus Van Tassel. The man's daughter, Katrina, was with him. It was love at first sight for Ichabod."

Alex broke in. "I thought you said this was a *ghost* story."

"Alex," Mrs. Chapman warned. "Let Mrs. Sullivan tell the story."

"Katrina had many admirers." Mrs. Sullivan went on. "One was Brom Van Brunt, nicknamed Brom Bones because he was so big and strong. Brom didn't like Ichabod. He wasn't about to let a scrawny schoolteacher win Katrina's heart."

Mrs. Sullivan took a sip of her lemonade. "On Halloween night, old Baltus Van Tassel had a big party. Everyone in the village came. There were food and drink and music. Ichabod danced with Katrina. That made Brom angry. When the dance was over, it was story-telling time. Brom told about the Headless Horseman."

Mattie's stomach quivered. A rider without a head!

"The Headless Horseman had been a Hessian soldier in the Revolutionary War," said Mrs. Sullivan. "The Hessians were Germans who fought on the British side. This particular Hessian lost his head to a cannon-ball! His body was buried in the graveyard, but some nights the Headless Hessian rode his ghost horse through Sleepy Hollow."

Mattie wished it wasn't so dark in the Keeping Room.

"Ichabod Crane didn't like this story," Mrs. Sullivan said. "He left the party to go home.

His knees were shaking so hard, he could barely get on his horse. He rode through the haunted woods, jumping at every little sound. He thought about the goblins in the woods. He thought about the Headless Horseman."

Mrs. Sullivan's voice grew louder. "Suddenly, a black horse galloped out of the woods! Its rider was headless! Ichabod spurred his own horse. Off they flew with the ghost behind him. Ichabod saw the haunted bridge. If he could make it across, the Headless Horseman would turn to dust. Ichabod raced across the bridge. He turned around—and saw the ghost rider hurl his head at him!"

"Wow!" Alex said. "Then what happened?"

"The next day, the villagers went to the bridge," said Mrs. Sullivan. "They found Ichabod's hat and a smashed pumpkin. Ichabod Crane was never seen again."

"Me and Ellsworth liked that story," said Sophie, clapping.

"It's 'The Legend of Sleepy Hollow,'" said Mr. Chapman. "I read it in high school. You changed it."

"Storytellers don't always tell stories the same way," Mrs. Sullivan said. "For me, it depends on who is listening, where I am, and the mood."

"So," asked Alex. "Did that Ichabod guy die or what? Did the ghost kill him?

Mrs. Sullivan spread her hands. "I don't know. What do you think?

Mattie gave a short laugh. "There aren't any ghosts. Everybody knows that." But she couldn't shake the funny feeling crawling up her spine.

Mrs. Chapman turned on the lamps. "It's getting late. Off to bed, kids."

In her room, Mattie heard a strange sound. *Scritch-scritch*. *Scritch-scritch*.

Something was scratching at her bedroom door. Maybe Winchester wanted in. She got up and opened the door.

A monster stood there, its horrible features eerily lit by a strange orange light.

Mattie shrieked. The monster started to laugh.

"Alex!" She snatched the flashlight her brother held under his chin. "*Not* funny!"

"You should see your face!" Alex said. "This flashlight is pretty handy."

Mattie shoved the flashlight at him. "Does it show you the way to *your* room?" She slammed her door and went back to bed.

The sound of rain dripping from the downspout outside her window woke Mattie. One look at the dark, overcast sky and she knew it would rain all day.

She dressed in jeans and a long-sleeved T-shirt. The mountains were chilly on rainy days, even in the summer.

Downstairs, she caught up to Alex as he headed into the dining room. He was also wearing jeans and a warm T-shirt. Mattie saw Mrs. Sullivan and hurried to sit next to her. Alex took the seat across from their new Travel Guide.

Sophie skipped into the room, twirling her green satin skirt and flapping the purple moon-and-stars cape.

"Sophie the Witch is joining us for breakfast," said Mrs. Sullivan.

"Was that story true?" Alex asked, helping himself to a piece of cinnamon toast. "The one you told us last night?"

Mrs. Sullivan poured cream into her coffee. "It was written by a man named Washington

Irving. Irving based his story on the old tales he'd heard all his life."

"But it's not true," Mattie insisted. "Ghosts and goblins aren't real."

"Ancient people believed in unseen spirits," Mrs. Sullivan said, heaping eggs and bacon onto her plate. "These stories helped them make sense of the natural world. They made up stories and created superstitions to explain things they didn't understand."

"I don't understand math," Alex said. "Do you think my teacher will let me make up a story instead?"

Mrs. Sullivan laughed. "I doubt it. Do you have any postcards?"

Mattie jumped up and fetched a postcard from the sideboard. Their next mission was about to start!

When Travel Guides left a postcard, the photo of the Gray Horse Inn would magically disappear and a new picture would give the kids a hint as to where they were going.

"What's stuperstitches?" asked Sophie, playing with the bow on Ellsworth's cape.

"*Superstitions*." Mattie corrected. "It means good luck and bad luck. But that stuff is just for little kids."

Mrs. Sullivan leaned over to show them a coin on a gold chain around her neck.

"I found this penny the day I met my husband. It was lying in a parking lot, heads up. That means it's good luck. And it was! I always wear it." She checked her watch. "I'd better get on the road."

She dropped the postcard in the silver mail tray and left the dining room. Mattie leaped up and grabbed the postcard. Alex and Sophie crowded around her.

"Let's see the picture," Alex said.

Mattie gasped. "I hope we're not going *there*!"

"Cool!" said Alex. "What's the message say?"

Mattie flipped the card over and read:

> Meet me here at the full of the moon and I'll whisper poetry in your ear. —I.C.

"Ew! Ick!" Alex said. Then he brightened. "Maybe this I.C. person was really going to scare somebody in that graveyard! Let's go!"

Mattie put the postcard back in the tray. She glanced at the spooky picture again. Was that mist wrapped around the tombstone? Or was it a ghost?

She shook her head and told herself, I *don't believe in ghosts*. Then why did she feel a tremor of fear?

"Come *on*," Alex said impatiently.

They ran up the stairs to the third floor. Alex knelt by the low, two-shelf bookcase and pushed on one edge. The bookcase swiveled inward and Alex crawled through the opening. Sophie and Mattie followed. Inside the tower room, they stood up. Rain streamed against the tall narrow windows.

Alex ran over to the desk, the only piece of furniture in the room. He removed a wooden box from a secret compartment. Lifting the lid, he took out a wooden spyglass.

"Ready?" he said, holding the spyglass by one end.

Sophie clasped the spyglass in the middle. Her purple cape fell over her shoulder.

"Wait!" Mattie said. "Sophie, you can't wear that Halloween costume."

"Yes, I can!" Sophie pushed out her bottom lip.

"If you don't change, we'll leave without you."

"No, you won't," said Sophie. "It's the rule."

Mattie frowned. Sophie was right—if they all didn't go, none of them could go.

"We're wasting time," Alex said. "The old church and graveyard in the postcard are pretty spooky. Sophie will probably fit right in."

"I doubt it," Mattie said. "I just hope we don't get into trouble." She reached for the other end of the spyglass.

Her fingers tingled as the spyglass grew warm. Strange symbols appeared on the extenders. She heard Alex speaking, faintly.

"Guess what?" she thought she heard him say. "I brought my flashlight!"

Before Mattie could reply, the floor dissolved under her feet. She whirled through a tunnel while sparks of orange, green, and purple light flickered behind her eyelids.

Then—*whomp*!—she landed.

3

Magic Ellsworth

"Ai-i-e-e-e-e-e-e!"

The scream filled Mattie's ears. She opened her eyes. Alex and Sophie appeared beside her.

They had definitely not landed in a Halloween party. Instead they stood in a cabin made from rough boards. Books, slates, benches, and a strange-looking map were tossed in the middle of the plank floorboards.

Although bright sun streamed through the single window, chilly air drifted in through the open door.

Who is screaming? Mattie wondered.

Then she saw a tall, skinny man perched on top of a stool. His bony knees poked up toward his ears. He clutched a blanket up to frightened green eyes. Mattie thought he looked like a giant grasshopper.

"You put a storm spell on my schoolroom!" the man said. He lowered the blanket and pointed a trembling finger at Sophie. "You're a witch!"

The man wore knee britches, white stockings, buckled shoes, and a long jacket. His reddish hair was tied back with a black ribbon. Mattie wondered if they had gone back to Colonial times again. On their first mission they had traveled to the time of the Revolutionary War.

Alex spoke first, "Our little sister is a pest sometimes, but she's hardly a witch."

"How else do you explain the child's garb?" the man insisted. "Her cloak is embroidered with hex symbols!"

"Hex symbols?" said Mattie. "Oh. Sophie's cape is part of a costume. The stars and moons are just decorations."

Now the man stared at her. "You're a witch too. And so is the boy. All of you descended in a cloud of magic. You can't tell me otherwise!"

Mattie looked at Alex. For the first time, they had arrived with someone watching. Normally they appeared in a place with no one else around, or in a crowd so large, they weren't noticed.

She glanced at the open front door. "We ran in the door. You didn't see us. We're just kids—children. Honest."

The man unfolded his long legs from the stool and stood up. "If you aren't witches, then that strange cloaked doll must be bad magic!"

Sophie held up her stuffed elephant. "This is Ellsworth. She's my best friend. She won't hurt anybody."

The man looked suspiciously at Ellsworth. Then he sighed. "The doll *seems* harmless."

Mattie had never seen such a scaredy-cat.

She tried to make him feel better. "I'm Mattie Chapman and this is my brother Alex."

The man studied her a moment, and then relaxed. Mattie wondered if he thought they were harmless too.

"I'm Ichabod Crane," he said.

As he came forward, Mattie bit back a giggle. He was so funny looking, with ears that stuck out and a big nose. And he was so skinny he could have been made out of pipe cleaners.

"I'm the village schoolmaster," Ichabod added.

Mattie nudged Alex. He nodded.

They had landed in Sleepy Hollow, in the ghost story their Travel Guide had told them! Stories, Mattie knew, could be even scarier than real life. On one of their adventures, they had climbed a beanstalk above the clouds and had been chased by a giant.

"Your room is a big mess," Sophie said to Ichabod.

"I walked my youngest student home," Ichabod said. "When I came back here, everything had been upset!"

"Who did it?" asked Mattie.

"Witches!" Ichabod exclaimed. "They hold meetings in my schoolhouse!"

"Really?" said Alex. Then he said, "Maybe the wind blew your stuff around. The door is open."

"The wind can't push over heavy benches. Besides, it's as still as a grave outside."

Mattie shivered at Ichabod's choice of words. "Maybe it was one of your boy students. You know how they can be," she added, remembering Alex's flashlight trick.

"This isn't the first time my schoolroom has been wrecked," said Ichabod. "If some of my students were playing pranks, I would have caught them. I'm sure this is the work of witches. Or perhaps goblins."

"You don't really believe in witches and goblins," Mattie said scornfully.

"The coves of Sleepy Hollow are filled with restless spirits. The woods are haunted by strange inhabitants." Ichabod lowered his voice. "And they are all after *me*."

"Why you?" asked Alex. "I mean, if these spirits really exist."

"They don't like me," Ichabod replied.

Mattie would have laughed except he looked so serious. "There aren't any ghosts or goblins or witches. It's just your imagination."

A shadow fell over the room, blotting out the bright sun.

"Be careful what you say!" Ichabod warned. "The trees have ears. And I wouldn't make fun of the spirits of Sleepy Hollow. Not if you want to live long."

Mattie gulped. She remembered the picture of the tombstone on the postcard and the strange message that ended, "You living men come view the ground where you must shortly lie."

"Listen," Alex said to Ichabod, "if you see a ghost, just yell at him and he'll go away."

Ichabod's green eyes widened. "Yell at a spirit? Are you mad, young man?" Then the corners of his mouth turned down. "I can't even shout at a field mouse. I'm the biggest coward in Sleepy Hollow."

"We won't let any ghosts get you," said Sophie. "Me and Ellsworth are real brave."

"We'll help you clean up," Alex offered. He picked up an overturned bench.

Matttie and Sophie collected books and slates. They stacked them on Ichabod's desk.

Ichabod carefully smoothed a map. "This map cost me a small fortune."

"What country is it?" asked Alex.

Ichabod raised his eyebrows in surprise. "Why, it's the United States of America."

Mattie stared at the thick parchment. It didn't look much like the United States. Only about half the states were colored. The rest of the country wasn't filled in.

Ichabod looked at her, then at Mattie and Alex. "I've never seen you children before. You don't go to my school. Where are you from?"

"Um—" Mattie hesitated. This was always the trickiest part of going back in time.

"We're from Virginia," answered Alex.

"Virginia!" Ichabod sounded astonished. "That state is hundreds of miles from New York! How did you get here?"

"We rode," said Mattie. Well, they did, sort of. Going back in time was always a wild ride.

"That's quite a journey on horseback," Ichabod said. "What brings you to Sleepy Hollow?"

"We came to see our aunt," replied Alex. "She lives in the next town. But we got lost."

"Your aunt lives in Croton? So you have no place to stay."

Mattie shook her head.

"I can take care of that," said Ichabod. "As schoolmaster, I stay with the families of my students. One week with one family, the next week with another. This week I'm staying with the Martling family. You can sleep in the Martlings' barn."

"Do they have cows?" asked Sophie. "I like cows."

"They have a very nice cow," Ichabod said. "Let's go saddle up Gunpowder. He'll be ready for his evening oats, I'm sure."

They walked outside the schoolhouse.

Ichabod latched the door with a heavy wooden bar.

A chilly breeze stirred the gold and red leaves. Mattie was glad she had worn jeans and long-sleeved shirt. It was fall here, not summer. And she was even glad Sophie was wearing that ridiculous costume. At least it was warm.

Ichabod strode to a clearing beside the schoolhouse, heading toward a post. He stopped and whirled in one direction, then the other.

"What is it?" Mattie asked.

"My horse!" he cried. "Gunpowder is gone!"

"Maybe he ran away," Alex suggested.

"I tied him firmly to that post. He couldn't have gotten free." Then Ichabod stared at Sophie, who was skipping around the clearing with Ellsworth.

Her purple moon-and-star cape fluttered behind her. Her long blond hair streamed in the breeze like a horse's tail. She hummed a theme song from a TV show.

"I knew it!" Ichabod exclaimed. "Sophie's doll! It has cast a spell over my horse. The doll *is* magic!"

4

Brom Bones

Mattie put her hands on her hips. If Ichabod was always scared, they'd never get anywhere.

"Don't be so superstitious!" she said to him. "Sophie's toy is perfectly ordinary."

"No, she's not," said Sophie. "Ellsworth is very special."

Mattie shot her sister a warning glance.

"Perhaps there are no evil spirits where you come from," Ichabod said. "But you would be wise to be cautious here."

"Are you kidding?" Alex blurted. "Virginia is filled with ghosts. You can't go down the street without tripping over one. Or walking through one, I mean."

"It's getting late," Mattie said hastily. "Sophie is hungry."

"You're right," said Ichabod. "Night falls quickly this time of year. We don't want to be caught in the forest after dark. The road is on the other side of the woods."

He led the way to a trail winding between enormous oaks and maples. A round moon rose over the treetops, white as a skull. Dead leaves skittered ahead of them as if kicked by invisible boots.

Ichabod scuttled down the trail, his eyes darting from side to side. Mattie wanted to laugh. If only he could see himself!

Just then a tiny reddish animal scurried

across their path. The creature disappeared in the bushes.

"Ah-ahhh!" Ichabod screeched, jumping a foot off the ground. "A monster!"

"That was a *chipmunk*," Mattie told him. "Nobody is afraid of a chipmunk."

Ichabod ducked his head sheepishly. "Didn't I tell you I am the biggest coward in Sleepy Hollow?"

Sophie put her hand on his arm. "That's okay. The chipmunk ran very fast."

As they walked farther into the woods, Ichabod whispered, "See that rock? There's a troll hidden inside."

Mattie squinted at the rock in the fading light. She could make out the faint outlines of a craggy nose, a scraggly beard. The rock *did* look like a troll!

Soon she heard the sound of water. A dark stream rushed between steep banks.

"The brook is haunted," said Ichabod. "If you fall in, you may never be seen again."

Two logs spanned the creek as a rough bridge. Ichabod crossed first, guiding Sophie. Then Alex scampered over the log.

When it was Mattie's turn, she stared down at the black water. What if she fell in? What would happen to her?

"Come *on*," Alex called.

Mattie climbed up on one of the logs and teetered to the other side, holding her arms out for balance. She hopped off in relief.

"How far is it to that farmer's house?" Alex asked Ichabod. "I'm hungry too."

"Not far, once we are on the road. If we make it to the road." He shuddered. "The spirits in these woods may wake and keep us from our destination."

"What do the spirits look like?" Mattie

wanted to know. Not that she believed in such things.

"Ghosts can take many forms. But they usually rise up like mist or fog." Ichabod sped up the pace. "We must hurry."

Mattie followed close on his heels. She shivered, not from the cold, but from Ichabod's stories.

Overhead, the bone-white moon grinned down at them. It wasn't dark, but it felt like midnight. The witching hour.

From deep in the woods came a weird cry. *Whip-whip-whip-poor-will*!

"Ahh-AHH!" Ichabod covered his head with his lanky arms.

Alex froze. "What was *that*?" he cried. "A goblin?"

"A goblin!" Mattie said in disgust. "It's a whip-poor-will. We hear those birds back home all the time."

"Yeah. I knew that," Alex said with a nervous laugh.

But Mattie couldn't shake the feeling that the woods were definitely creepy. Anything could be possible in a spooky place like this. No wonder Ichabod and even Alex were scared!

At last the path led them to a wide road. Ichabod pointed north and they began walking. After a few minutes, Ichabod slowed his pace. Mattie noticed a huge tree with two intertwined trunks growing in the center of the road. Gnarled branches, as big as trees themselves, twisted downward, nearly touching the ground.

"This tree is especially haunted," Ichabod whispered as they crept around it. "A British soldier named Major Andre was captured by American soldiers. It is said he was hung as a spy from the very limbs of this tree."

When one of the low-hanging branches clawed at Alex's head, he shrieked.

"What's *with* you?" Mattie said. But she walked way around the haunted tree.

A clattering sound made them both turn. A carriage drew up beside them. It was pulled by four sleek black horses and driven by a uniformed coachman. Red velvet curtains draped the windows.

A hand pushed one of the curtains aside. A man with a bushy brown beard leaned out of the carriage and called, "Hello, Mr. Crane! Out for a stroll?"

Ichabod opened his mouth to answer just as the other curtain was pulled back. A pretty girl with blond curls waved at him. Then the coachman flicked the reins and the carriage rattled past.

Ichabod gazed after it, his mouth still open. He didn't move.

"Earth to Ichabod," Alex said, snapping his fingers in Ichabod's face. "Hello?"

"What?" Ichabod started.

"Who was that girl?" Mattie asked.

"Her name is Katrina," he replied with a sigh. "She's the daughter of Baltus Van Tassel. Old Baltus is the wealthiest man in Sleepy Hollow."

"You like her," Sophie said to him.

"Yes," said Ichabod in a faraway voice. "I do."

In the moonlight, Mattie could see his dreamy expression. Remembering Mrs. Sullivan's story, she whispered to Alex, "We have to help him get Katrina to like him back. That's our mission."

"Blech!" was Alex's reply.

"We'd better hurry or we'll miss supper at Farmer Martling's," said Ichabod.

They walked down the road, which was

bordered with low stone walls and fences. Once, they saw a boy leading a cow on a rope across a pasture.

Mattie stumbled over a loose stone. She was tired and hungry. She hoped the farmer's wife was a good cook.

Then Mattie felt the ground beneath her feet begin to vibrate. She heard hoofbeats thundering behind them. Mattie leaped to the side of the road, dragging Sophie with her. Alex jumped into the ditch.

An enormous black horse thudded powerfully toward them. A giant half-stood in the stirrups. The horse nearly galloped over Ichabod before plowing to a stop.

"Well, if it isn't the schoolmaster!" the man bellowed. "Out kind of late, aren't you? Aren't you afraid ghosties and goblins will get you?"

Studying the man closely, Mattie realized

he wasn't a real giant. But he was definitely the biggest man she'd ever seen. His arms were the size of hams and he could have carried a person on each broad shoulder. Ichabod looked like a toothpick.

"Hello, Brom," Ichabod said. Mattie could tell by his voice he was pretending to be polite. "Children, may I introduce Mr. Van Brunt."

"Call me Brom Bones," the black-haired stranger said.

"Brom Bones is the coolest name!" said Alex.

Brom looked puzzled. Mattie wished Alex would remember they were back in the eighteen hundreds. People used the word "cool" when they talked about the weather.

Then Brom turned back to Ichabod. "How come you're riding shank's mare?"

"Whose mare?" said Alex.

"Shank's mare means to walk," Ichabod

said. To Brom, he added stiffly, "It's a nice evening for a walk."

Brom threw back his head and laughed. The sound boomed, breaking the stillness of the evening.

"I think you misplaced that broken-down nag of yours," he said with a sneer. "Getting absentminded, aren't you, professor? One of these days, you may lose your *head*!" He laughed again.

Ichabod flinched as if he had been struck.

Mattie knew he was afraid of Brom Bones, but who wouldn't be? The guy was a big bully.

"I suppose you know the whereabouts of my horse?" Ichabod said stiffly.

Brom put one finger against his temple, as if he were thinking hard. "You know, I believe I saw a nag just like yours earlier today."

"Just tell me," said Ichabod.

"Look where the Headless One goes! If you dare!"

With that, Brom jerked the reins and wheeled his stallion around.He galloped down the road, his harsh laughter lingering long after he vanished from sight.

Then Mattie heard another sound. Ichabod's teeth were chattering.

"What is it?" she asked.

"G-gunpowder," he stammered. "B-brom must have taken my horse to the b-burying ground!"

5

The Headless Horseman

You mean the graveyard?" said Alex. "So what?"

Ichabod stared at him. "Now is not the time to explain. We must hurry before the hour grows any later."

He half-jogged down the road. His arms moved so fast, Mattie thought he would take flight. He even looked like a bird, with his beaky nose and stork-like legs.

Soon they came upon an old brick building tucked in a curve in the road. Its white steeple gleamed in the twilight, but the arched windows were dark, like empty eyes.

"The Old Dutch Church," Ichabod whispered.

Just around the bend was a graveyard. In the tall grass, tombstones leaned this way and that. Scraps of mist flowed around the old marble markers like scarves. With a jolt, Mattie realized this was the scene on the Travel Guide's postcard.

A chestnut horse was tied to a tree branch. He whinnied nervously when he saw them, swishing his tail.

Ichabod clucked his tongue. "Poor Gunpowder. He's half out of his wits with fear." He quickly untied the horse and led him to the road.

"Can Sophie ride him?" Mattie asked. "She's tired."

Ichabod lifted Sophie into the saddle. "The rest of us can walk. It's not far."

"Now will you tell us?" asked Alex. "About that graveyard?"

Ichabod led the horse a few minutes before he answered. "If this were the witching hour, we would be in terrible danger! Unhappy spirits lie in the burying ground. They often rise from their graves to wander the country-side. But everyone is afraid of one particular spirit: The Headless Hessian!"

"Have you ever seen him?" Sophie asked.

"No! And I hope I never do!" Ichabod lowered his voice. "He fought with the British in the Rebellion. A cannonball claimed his head. He was buried in the churchyard. At night, he leaves his grave and gallops his phantom horse in search of his head. He rides like a fury, because he must return to the burying ground before daybreak or he will turn to dust."

"That's only superstition," Mattie said. But a chill rippled down her spine. She knew it was only a story, but it sounded different here in Sleepy Hollow.

This place should be called Creepy Hollow, she thought.

They passed a large yellow-brick house. The Van Tassel carriage stood beside the house. A massive black horse grazed beside the iron hitching post. Brom's horse.

"Brom is visiting Katrina," Ichabod said sadly. "I don't have a chance with her now. Brom is everything I am not—strong, quick, and brave."

"I bet he's not as smart as you are," said Mattie.

"Intelligence doesn't matter when you're Brom Bones," said Ichabod, moving on.

The house next to the Van Tassels' was much smaller. Warm light poured from the windows. A red barn had been built close to the road.

"Farmer Martling left the barn door open," said Ichabod, tying Gunpowder to a hitching post near the barn. "I'll bring your supper in a few minutes."

"Aren't we eating in the house with you?" Mattie asked.

Ichabod helped Sophie down from the horse. "Um . . . I think it's best you stay out of sight for now." He left to go inside the house.

The barn was pitch-black. Mattie stepped over the doorsill, her heart in her throat. As she stretched out her hand to feel her way, something large and wet touched it.

"Alex!" she shrieked. "There's a monster in here!"

Instantly the inside of the barn lit up. Alex

stood behind her, waving his flashlight.

"Are you crazy?" Mattie exclaimed. "Turn that thing off!"

"You were the one who screamed," he said. "There's your monster."

Sophie was across the barn, knee-deep in hay. Her arms were wrapped around the neck of a black and white cow. "Her name is Buttercup. Isn't she sweet?"

Mattie flushed with embarrassment. Scared by a cow! "Give me that flashlight, Alex. You shouldn't have brought it back to the olden days."

He switched off the flashlight and stuffed it in his pocket. "I won't use it again."

Mattie and Alex collapsed on a bale of hay. The cow mooed gently as Sophie murmured to her.

Alex's voice sounded hollow in the darkness. "I'm starving."

"Buttercup just ate," said Sophie. "She told me so."

"Great," Mattie said. "We're in Spooksville with a talking cow. If Ichabod knew that, he'd *really* have something to be scared of."

"I'm not crazy about this mission," Alex said. "Getting a girl to like a guy. I mean, how dumb!"

"I'm not crazy about this *place*," Mattie put in. "But we're here and we have to help make Katrina like Ichabod."

"And not that Brom guy," said Alex. "I bet Brom messed up Ichabod's school when he swiped his horse."

"I just thought of something," Mattie said. "Brom doesn't like Ichabod. Maybe *he's* the one who scared Ichabod by playing the Headless Horseman."

"Don't you think the Headless Horseman is real?" asked Alex. "I mean, this place must be crawling with ghosts."

"No, I don't think he's real. I think it's Brom playing another trick on Ichabod." At least she *hoped* it was Brom. To cover her doubts, Mattie became businesslike. "Any ideas how we can make Katrina like Ichabod?"

"He said he wants to be strong, quick, and brave like Brom Bones," said Alex.

"Let's do strong first," said Mattie. "But he's so skinny. Somehow we have to turn him into Super Ichabod."

"I know," Alex said. "We'll train him, like those guys who lift weights on TV. They get strong by lifting heavy things."

Ichabod slipped into the barn, carrying a basket and a lantern. He set the basket on a crate and hooked the lantern on a nail.

"I told Farmer Martling's wife that I'd rather eat in here," he said. "This basket is so heavy, it must be stuffed with food."

Mattie looked at Ichabod's twiggy arms and legs as he unpacked the basket. She wondered how they would ever make him as strong as Brom Bones.

Using a keg for a table, the kids dove into the meal—thick slices of ham and sugar doughnuts still warm from the frying pan. But Mattie and Alex only took a sip of the fresh, warm milk in the pewter pitcher. Sophie wouldn't even touch it.

"Eeew," Mattie said, holding her nose. "This milk is awful! It should be in the—" She stopped before she blurted the word *refrigerator*.

"Who cares?" said Alex, stuffing his third doughnut into his mouth. "These doughnuts are so good, I might stay in this time period forever."

Ichabod gawked at him. "What did you say?"

"Uh—he means, he might stay in this *barn* forever," Mattie said quickly. Then she added, "You know, Ichabod, if you began lifting things, you'd be as strong as Brom Bones. Katrina would think you had a lot of muscles."

"Really?" Ichabod flexed his bony arm. "I don't suppose it would hurt."

Alex rolled a heavy wooden bucket over to him. "Pick that up."

Ichabod lifted the bucket up to his waist.

"Higher," Mattie ordered. "Over your head!"

Groaning, Ichabod hefted the bucket above his head as if it were a thousand pounds. His knees knocked together with the effort. Then he dropped it on the hay-covered floor.

"Whew!" he said, wiping his forehead with his sleeve.

"That was pretty good," Mattie said, even though it wasn't. "But you have to do it at least a hundred times. That's how you build muscles."

"One hundred times!" Ichabod looked shocked. "How about fifty? Tomorrow morning?"

Mattie sighed. "All right."

He slipped back out the door, leaving them the lantern.

The kids piled hay in the middle of the barn to make beds. Sophie fixed her bed near Buttercup. Then she curled up with Ellsworth, spreading her purple cape like a blanket.

Mattie couldn't get comfortable. The hay was itchy.

"Alex," she said. "Do you believe in ghosts?"

But Alex was already asleep.

She lay awake, watching shadows flit across the wall like goblins. At last she drifted into an uneasy sleep.

The smell of something sweet and hot tickled Mattie's nose. She opened her eyes to see Ichabod unpacking another basket. He wore a black coat today with a white, high-collared shirt.

"Good morning," he said. "The farmer's wife made crullers today."

Alex crammed the sweet fried bread in his mouth before he was fully awake. "Mmmm! These are better than the doughnuts!"

"Are you ready to lift the bucket?" Mattie asked Ichabod. "You promised me you'd do it fifty times."

He flecked a piece of dust from his sleeve. "I can't get my jacket dirty. This is my best outfit."

"You can't be any stronger from lifting the bucket one time!"

"I think I am. I believe I could lift a calf," Ichabod declared.

This is going to be a tough mission, Mattie thought, fuming. *Ichabod Crane is stubborn.*

When they finished breakfast, Ichabod said, "We must go before the farmer's wife comes to turn the cow out to pasture."

"I can't leave Buttercup!" Sophie wailed. "We're best friends!"

"Don't be ridiculous, Sophie," said Mattie. "We have to *go.*"

Sniffling, Sophie hugged the cow good-bye, and then followed Mattie out the door.

As soon as they were out of the barn, Buttercup started mooing.

"Hurry!" Ichabod said, untying Gunpowder. "The farmer's wife will wonder what is upsetting her cow."

They began to run across the field. Mattie looked over her shoulder.

A red-faced chunky woman stepped out of the house. She wore an apron and a white-ruffled cap. The woman glared at the kids, especially Sophie.

Mattie gasped.

The farmer's wife was giving Sophie the evil eye!

6

The Witch Child

They rushed away from the barn, Ichabod leading Gunpowder. Mattie expected the farmer's wife to yell at Sophie but there was only stony silence behind them.

Alex walked beside her. "Did you see the way that lady looked at Sophie?"

Mattie nodded. "It was scary. This whole place is so creepy!"

On the other side of the barn was a

field. Cut cornstalks stood upright in papery bundles. Between the cornstalks grew orange pumpkins, gleaming gold in the autumn sunshine. A man in brown breeches heaved an enormous pumpkin into a cart. The cart was hitched to a big black horse.

Brom Bones grinned when he saw Ichabod. "Did you come to help load Farmer Martling's pumpkins?" he asked with a sneer.

"I'm feeling quite fit today," said Ichabod. "I'll be glad to help."

Mattie knew Ichabod wasn't a bit stronger. Not unless he'd been taking megavitamins.

Brom laughed and tossed a pumpkin at Ichabod. "Catch!"

"Oof!" The pumpkin hit Ichabod in the stomach and smashed on the ground.

"Farmer Martling won't have many pumpkins to take to market if you keep dropping them," said Brom.

"That wasn't fair!" Mattie exclaimed. "You tricked him!"

Brom ignored her. "There's only room in the cart for this last pumpkin," he said to Ichabod. "Be my guest."

The pumpkin he pointed to was the size of a car tire. Mattie figured it must have weighed three hundred pounds.

"You can do it!" Alex told Ichabod.

Ichabod stooped and put his scrawny arms around the giant pumpkin. Gritting his teeth, he struggled to pick it up. He toppled over, his legs waving in the air. He looked like a beetle on its back. The pumpkin hadn't budged.

"Weakling!" Brom jeered. He hefted the huge pumpkin as if it were a feather and set it easily on the cart. Then he went around front to check on his horse.

Mattie helped Ichabod to his feet. "What's

so great about being strong, anyway?"

"I agree," he said. Then he sighed.

"What about number two on the list?" Sophie said.

Ichabod frowned, puzzled. "What list?"

"You said you wanted to show Katrina you're quick," Mattie explained. "I bet you're a fast runner."

He nodded. "I ran foot races when I was a child. I always won."

"Runners are skinny guys," said Alex. "They don't need big muscles to go fast."

"Tell Bonehead over there you want to race him," Mattie said to Ichabod. "The race will start in front of the church at noon. And invite everyone to come. Katrina will see you beat Brom. You'll be her hero."

Alex made a gagging face.

Ichabod's green eyes lit up. "What a wonderful idea! I'll challenge Brom right now."

"And then," said Mattie, "we'll put you in training."

She'd been captain of her soccer team back when they lived in Maryland. She knew exactly how to get Ichabod Crane into shape.

Bright October sunshine bathed the Old Dutch Church in a yellow glow. Even the tombstones in the burying ground didn't seem as scary.

Many had strange carvings—simple round faces like Sophie might draw. The faces sprouted wings where ears should have been. Mattie paused in front of a fancy gravestone to read the faded inscription:

Evert Arser (died 1765, aged 22)
Hark from tomb a doleful voice
My ears attend the cry
You living men come view the ground
Where you must shortly lie

It seemed like a message from a grave. Mattie shivered in the warm sun.

"Matt!" Alex called from the other side of the cemetery. "Look!"

A group of people ambled down the road, led by Baltus Van Tassel. Brom Bones strolled arm in arm with Katrina Van Tassel.

"The whole village is coming to see the race!" Mattie said excitedly. "Where is Ichabod?"

"Behind the church with Sophie," Alex answered. "Doing those exercises you showed him."

The villagers stopped in front of the church and lined up along both sides of the road.

Brom stepped out of the crowd and looked at Mattie. "Did Mr. Crane back out?" he asked in his booming voice. Then he flapped his elbows and clucked like a chicken.

The villagers laughed.

"I did not back out!" Ichabod strode around the church, a handkerchief tied around his neck. He whipped the handkerchief off with a snap and said to Brom, "I'm ready if you are."

Mattie had scratched a line in the road in front of the church. She pointed to it with the toe of her sneaker.

"This is the starting mark," she said, loud enough so everyone could hear. "Run up the road to that big tree, turn around, come back down the road, go around the church, through the graveyard, and back to this mark."

"Runners!" he called. "Take your marks!"

Brom sidled over to the line and studied his fingernails. Mattie knew he was acting casual to make Ichabod nervous. Ichabod took his position next to Brom.

"Get on your marks!" Alex shouted, holding his arm out in front of Ichabod and Brom like a flag.

Ichabod hunkered down in the runner's stance Mattie had taught him. Brom stared at him.

"Get set!"

Ichabod's rear end bobbed into the air. Brom laughed so hard, he almost fell over. Everyone roared with laughter at the sight of Ichabod crouched like a giant spider.

"Go!" Alex dropped his arm.

The runners sprinted down the road, kicking up dirt. Brom easily took the lead, waving to the villagers as if he were in a parade.

Ichabod ran with his knees high like a circus pony, his bony arms churning the air. Instead of grinning at the crowd like Brom, he kept his eyes ahead. At the big tree, he dashed past Brom and grabbed the lead.

"Go, Ichabod!" Sophie cried, jumping up and down.

"You can do it!" Mattie yelled.

Ichabod ran as if he were being chased by all the goblins in the haunted woods. Brom's big legs pumped fast, but he still trailed behind.

"He's going to win!" Alex high-fived Mattie.

The runners circled the church. They had one part of the race left, through the old cemetery.

But as soon as Ichabod entered the graveyard, he slowed down, his eyes wide. He tiptoed around the tombstones.

"Run!" Mattie called to him.

Brom trotted up behind Ichabod and yelled, "Boo!"

Ichabod tripped over his own feet and tumbled over. He landed against the tombstone inscribed, "Where you must shortly lie."

Brom jogged to the finish line, thrusting his fists upward. "The champion!"

"You won!" Katrina cried, clapping.

Everyone in the audience cheered and applauded. Mattie, Alex, and Sophie didn't move. They couldn't believe Ichabod had lost the race.

Then Mattie stomped into the graveyard. "You let that big bully scare you!"

As Ichabod staggered to his feet, he didn't look at Mattie. Instead he gazed sadly across the road. Katrina was walking away with Brom.

Suddenly Mattie felt sorry for Ichabod. He would never be strong or quick like Brom. The only thing left was to make Ichabod brave and *that* was impossible. She sighed. They'd better get to work. They couldn't go home until they completed the mission.

Just then a woman in a white apron and cap pushed to the front of the crowd of villagers. Mattie recognized her as the farmer's wife. The woman pointed a plump finger at Sophie. A slight breeze had come up, stirring Sophie's purple star-and-moon cape.

"That girl!" the farmer's wife cried. "Don't let her get away! She's a witch child!"

7

Trouble!

A gasp rose from the crowd. Everyone stared at Sophie.

Mattie's stomach felt like Jell-O. She was really afraid for Sophie. But she didn't want the villagers to know she was terrified.

"Sophie is *not* a witch child," she said sternly. "She's a regular child!"

"She put a spell on my cow!" the farmer's wife declared.

Mattie noticed the woman had a big nose with an ugly mole. The woman looked more like a witch than Sophie did.

"I saw those children leaving my barn." The farmer's wife went on. "The little one waved that strange doll. And now my cow won't give milk!"

"Buttercup doesn't like the field you stick her in," Sophie said. "She told me she likes the other field. The one by the river."

"See?" the woman screeched. "The child talked to my cow!"

Sophie tossed her hair. "She'd talk to you but you're not nice to her. That's why Buttercup kicked you once."

"Nell Martling is right! That child *is* a witch!" cried another woman with wild black hair.

Mattie's heart sank. Sophie was usually shy around strangers. Why did she have to blab to the entire village that she could communicate with animals?

"What'll we do?" Alex whispered. He looked frightened too.

"I don't know." Mattie remembered what Mrs. Sullivan said about superstitions. When people didn't understand things, they made up stories.

How could she explain that Sophie *did* have a way with animals? But that didn't mean she was a witch. Sophie was different, but not in a bad way.

"She's even dressed like a witch," the farmer's wife said. "There are hex signs all over her cloak."

Mattie stepped between Sophie and Nell Martling. "Sophie is wearing a play outfit. It's my old Halloween costume, actually—"

The woman brought her hand up to her mouth in a gesture of horror. "All Hallow's Eve

78

is tonight! The child will join other witches and ride her broomstick across the sky!"

"No, she won't!" Alex yelled. "Leave my sister alone."

Farmer Martling, who'd been standing next to Baltus Van Tassel, suddenly spoke. "Who *are* these children? They speak oddly. They don't dress like we do. Where did they come from?"

"We came from Virginia," Mattie told him. Maybe everyone would calm down when they realized they weren't aliens from another planet.

"Virginia!" exclaimed the farmer. "Do girls wear men's pants down there? And how did these children get all the way from that country to our village?"

Mattie was stunned. They thought Virginia was another country! She flashed a desperate glance at Ichabod.

Ichabod nervously cleared his throat. "These children are traveling to meet their aunt in Croton. Only they lost their way. I was going to help them but . . ." His voice trailed off.

A harsh laugh broke the silence. Brom Bones stood there, hands on hips. Mattie thought he and Katrina had left, but they must have just taken a stroll.

"You? Help witches?" said Brom Bones. "You're scared of your own shadow! Aren't you afraid these children will put a spell on you?"

"Well . . . " Ichabod hesitated. "They seem harmless."

Mattie felt the prickle of anger. She shouldn't count on Ichabod Crane to be much help! Her temper boiled over.

"What's the matter with you people?" she yelled. "We *are* harmless!"

"Of course they are," spoke a new voice.

Katrina Van Tassel stepped forward. Her

blue-flowered gown swished over the grass. Beneath the brim of her blue velvet bonnet, blond curls gleamed in the sunlight. Her blue eyes looked kindly at Mattie.

"My father and I are giving a party tonight at our house," she said in her clear, sweet voice. "We would like everyone in the village to come."

Cheers rose from the crowd.

"What about them?" Nell Martling pointed to Mattie, Alex, and Sophie. "Do we dare leave them loose in the village while we are away from our homes, feasting and dancing?"

"The children shall come too," said Katrina.

A wave of relief swept over Mattie.

"That was close!" she whispered to Alex.

"You got that right," he whispered back. "For a while I thought they were going to lock us up in jail!"

Sophie smiled up at Katrina. "You're very pretty," she said. "And you don't have a big hairy bump on your nose." She looked over her shoulder at the farmer's wife.

The woman's cheeks turned almost as purple as Sophie's cape.

Mattie knew the farmer's wife had heard Sophie's remark. They needed to get out of there in case Sophie said something that landed them in worse trouble.

Sophie held Ellsworth up to Katrina. "Meet Ellsworth. She's my best friend in the whole world." Then she spoke to the stuffed elephant. "Guess what, Ellsworth? We're going to a Halloween party tonight!"

Mattie smacked her forehead. What *was* it with her sister today? Sophie was chattier than a parrot.

"Look!" the farmer's wife shrieked. "The witch child is talking to that strange doll!

The doll gives her magical powers!"

A murmur rushed through the crowd.

Mattie pulled Sophie to her side. "Be *quiet*," she said in a low tone. "Do not say another word!"

But it was too late.

"Witch child!" screamed the black-haired woman.

Farmer Martling pounded a fist into his palm. "I think *all* those kids are witches!"

"They sure aren't like the rest of us," Brom Bones agreed. "But then, neither is our friend Ichabod Crane."

Just then Baltus Van Tassel pushed through the mob. He stood in the clearing with both hands raised to get their attention.

"All right! All right!" he announced. "Let's not lose our heads over this."

"That happened once already," said Brom, and everyone snickered.

Baltus Van Tassel ignored his remark. "Since the whole village is invited to our house tonight, why don't we decide then what we will do with these children, particularly the little one?"

Sophie ducked behind Mattie.

"It's all right, Soph," Mattie whispered. "We won't let anybody hurt you."

"I'm not afraid for me." Sophie's voice was very small. "They might take Ellsworth!"

"Let 'em try," Alex said.

But Mattie was worried. They needed to solve this mission and get home quick, before there were three more graves in the burying ground.

8

Creepy Hollow

"Who'll watch those children until the party this evening?" said Farmer Martling. "We must get back to our fields."

Ichabod raised his hand. "I will."

As the villagers left, Brom said to Ichabod, "Hope the children don't put a spell on you. It would be a *shame* if you couldn't make it to the party tonight."

"I'll be there," Ichabod told him. "Come on, children."

He led them through the woods to the schoolhouse. His long face sagged with gloom.

Mattie knew he was disappointed because he had lost the race. So far Brom Bones was the strongest and fastest. That left courage. How could they make the biggest chicken in the world suddenly brave as a lion?

"I must go into the village for a while," Ichabod said, opening the door of the school-house. "Will you be all right until I come back for you?"

"We'll be fine," said Alex.

"I'm going to latch the door," said Ichabod. "Not because I think you'll leave. I don't want any of the villagers to bother you."

As soon as she heard the wood bar *thunk* across the door, Mattie pulled up the stool and sat down.

"Okay," she said in a business-like tone. "We've only got a few hours to come up with a plan to make Ichabod brave."

Alex snorted. "We'd need, like, twenty years to do that. Maybe longer!"

"We must finish the mission," Mattie said, "and leave Creepy Hollow before Sophie gets us in worse trouble."

"I didn't do anything," Sophie said.

"You told everyone what the cow said to you! You wore that ridiculous outfit!" Then Mattie stopped. Sophie was right. It wasn't her fault the villagers thought she was a witch.

"The people here are really weird," Alex said. "The stuff they believe in!"

"Okay, we have to focus. We know Brom is going to pretend to be the Headless Horseman and scare Ichabod after the party. What can we do to stop him?"

"I know!" Alex said. "We'll find Brom's costume and the pumpkin and show Ichabod. That'll fix Brom."

Mattie chewed a strand of hair. "But that won't make Ichabod look brave or Katrina like him any better. Ichabod has to *show up* that bully Brom, not just mess up his plan."

"Change it," Sophie said.

"Change what?" Mattie asked, frowning.

"The story. Mrs. Sullivan said we could."

Just like in cartoons, Mattie felt a lightbulb switch on over her head.

"Hey!" she said. "What if *another* ghost was out tonight? One a lot scarier than the Headless Horseman?"

"What could be scarier than a guy with no head?" asked Alex.

Mattie grinned. "Gather 'round, listeners, and I'll tell you a new ending to an old story."

Mattie peeked around the corner of the big stone house. She heard voices talking. Delicious smells wafted from the kitchen. People in the Van Tassel house were probably getting ready for the party. Then Mattie looked back where Alex and Sophie were hiding in the ditch by the road. She waved, signaling that the coast was clear.

Alex ran up to the house, carrying a bundle. Sophie scampered after him.

"Around back," Mattie whispered hoarsely. "Hurry! Somebody's coming!"

They dashed to a tree stump behind the house and waited, breathless.

A wagon pulled up the lane beside the house. The driver hopped down, and then lifted a heavy wooden keg off the wagon. He rolled the keg into the house.

"We can leave it here," Mattie whispered, flattening the bundle. "Nobody will see it."

Quickly, before the driver came out of the house, the kids sprinted across the lawn, over the road, and into the woods. They soon found the path that led back to the schoolhouse. They climbed through the window and sat down on the benches, as if they'd never left.

Minutes later, the door was unlatched and Ichabod walked in. He looked very serious.

Mattie jumped up. "Guess what? We've figured out a way—"

Ichabod held up his hand. He cleared his throat, and then said, "I have some distressing news. Tonight at the party there's going to be a sort of trial."

"What do you mean, 'a sort of'?" asked Alex.

"It won't be a real trial," Ichabod replied hastily, "with a judge and jury. The villagers will decide what to do with you."

Mattie thought that sounded more frightening than a real trial.

"Aren't you going to help us?" she demanded. "Are you going to let them believe we're witches?"

But all Ichabod said was, "It's time to go. Sophie will ride Gunpowder. We'll walk."

Outside, a huge pumpkin-colored moon floated over the treetops. Mattie had never seen such a big moon. It tilted toward the earth and looked like it was laughing.

She didn't feel like laughing back. What would happen at the trial? Suppose the villagers found the spyglass and took it away from them? The spyglass was their only way back home.

As they walked through the woods, Ichabod trembled at every rustling leaf. *He'll be no help*, Mattie thought.

The Van Tassel house was lit from top

to bottom like an enormous jack-o'-lantern. Laughter, loud voices, and fiddle music poured from the house.

Ichabod strode up the paved walk. The front door swung open and he went inside, with the kids following. Instantly, the noise died.

Among the crowd, Mattie recognized Baltus Van Tassel and Katrina. She saw Brom Bones and Farmer Martling and his wife. She felt the icy glare of all the party guests and shivered.

"Here they are!" bellowed Farmer Martling. "Let's get on with the trial!"

The others took up the cry. "The trial!"

"Just a minute!" Baltus Van Tassel held up a hand. "This is a party. I want everyone to enjoy food and drink. At nine o'clock, we'll talk about these children."

Mattie glanced at a clock across the room.

Eight o'clock. They had exactly one hour to accomplish their mission. If they failed . . . she didn't want to think about that.

Alex strolled by with a pewter plate piled high with sugary doughnuts.

"What are you doing?" Mattie asked.

"Eating. The guy said everybody should eat." He licked his lips with delight and bit into a doughnut.

Mattie went into the dining room. The table groaned under pewter platters of sliced ham, roasted chickens, fried fish, apple and pumpkin pies, and dishes of nuts and dried fruits. Cloth-wrapped baskets of doughnuts and crullers stood on a writing desk.

Brom Bones pushed by Mattie as he loaded a plate with ham, pumpkin pie, a whole chicken, and a fistful of crullers.

Mattie noticed Ichabod talking to Katrina, who laughed at something he said.

Then Ichabod slipped a note into Katrina's hand. She read it and blushed.

"I don't know if I can get away from the party," Katrina said.

I *bet he asked her to meet him at the church tonight*, Mattie thought, remembering the postcard message. If Katrina met Ichabod and they hit it off, they wouldn't have to finish this mission.

But then Brom saw Ichabod and Katrina. His face grew red. Mattie worried he might pick a fight with Ichabod.

Instead he announced, "Did I ever tell anyone how I outran the Headless Horseman?"

"No!" said Baltus. "Tell!"

Brom set his plate down. "One Halloween I was riding back from Croton when I saw the Headless Hessian. I challenged him to a race to the old bridge. We were off!"

"What happened?" Katrina asked.

"Through the woods his ghostly steed ran," Brom continued, waving his hands dramatically. "But my horse Daredevil was faster."

Mattie looked at Ichabod. In the dancing candlelight, his face had turned a sickly shade of green. She knew he didn't like this story.

"I should have beat the spirit fair and square," Brom said. "But when we got to the bridge, he vanished in a blaze of lightning! Poof!" He leaped as he spoke the last word.

Ichabod shrank.

"Does that story frighten you?" Brom asked Ichabod.

"N-no," Ichabod said. "It's—just a tale. As a matter of fact, I could ride through the woods to the old bridge tonight."

Brom threw back his head and laughed.

"Scaredy-cat Crane go out on the night the Headless One rides?"

"It's true," said Ichabod. "I'll go now and come back to show you I'm not afraid of … of …"

He couldn't even say the words *Headless Horseman*, Mattie realized. He really needed their help. She had to tell him their plan.

She looked at the writing desk and got an idea. First she tore off a tiny piece of parchment paper. Then, using a quill dipped in ink, she jotted a message. She rolled the paper into a tight tube and poked it in the middle of a doughnut.

"Eat this," she said to Ichabod, handing him the doughnut. "*Carefully*."

Ichabod took a bite of the doughnut and found the paper. He read the message and nodded.

Outside, people gathered on the porch to watch Ichabod climb on Gunpowder.

"Don't get too scared and fall off!" laughed Farmer Martling.

His face pale in the lamplight, Ichabod turned Gunpowder toward the road, and then disappeared into the raven-dark woods.

The villagers went back inside. Mattie saw Brom slip around to the back of the house. She motioned to Alex and Sophie and they all followed him. Brom stooped behind a tree and pulled out a long black cloak and a pumpkin. He put the pumpkin into a sack. Then he mounted his horse Daredevil and clattered down the road after Ichabod.

"That stinker," said Alex. "He's going to play Headless Horseman."

"Yeah, but he won't be alone," Mattie said. "Fetch our bundle. Let's get out of here."

The kids crept along the side of the house so no one would see them. When they reached the road, they walked toward the Old Dutch

Church, in the direction Ichabod and Brom had ridden.

The harvest moon had climbed higher in the sky and was now a cold, ghostly white. Fog shrouded their feet as they stumbled down the road.

Mattie felt her mouth go dry. She wondered if maybe the old stories were right, that there really *were* ghosts.

Then . . . out of the drifting fog loomed a large, dark shape. It gave a low, unearthly cry.

— 9 —

The Ghost Rides Again

"Buttercup!" Sophie exclaimed.

The cow's big head appeared over the fence. She mooed again and Sophie spoke softly to her.

"The farmer's wife forgot to put Buttercup in the barn tonight," Sophie explained.

"That cow scared me half to death," Mattie said, dizzy with relief.

Sophie patted the cow's neck. "We can use

Buttercup in our plan. She'll let us."

"Sophie's right," Alex said, shifting the bundle. "We need her."

Mattie thought it over. "Buttercup will make our plan much better."

Alex opened the gate and Sophie led the cow out by a rope around Buttercup's neck. Then they continued down the road.

When they reached the double tree in the middle of the road, Alex said, "The British spy was hung here. I wonder if his ghost will be walking tonight."

"Thanks, Alex!" Mattie said. "The last thing I need to hear about is another ghost!"

"But you don't believe in them."

"It's different here. Everything is different in Creepy Hollow."

They crossed the road to the path in the woods. The woods were inky black, except for the ghostly fog that draped the bushes. Bats squeaked overhead and small animals skittered in the dead leaves.

Mattie stopped. "Listen!"

Crash! *Slash*!

Something big thrashed through the underbrush. Hoofbeats thrummed against the ground.

"Horses!" said Alex. "Heading our way."

"Ai-i-i-e-e-e!" came a horrible scream.

"Ichabod!" Mattie said. "Brom must be after him, pretending to be the Headless Horseman."

"We'd better hurry," said Alex.

Mattie stood uncertainly next to the cow. "Sophie, are you sure she won't buck or anything?"

"Buttercup wouldn't hurt an ant."

Mattie clutched fistfuls of Buttercup's hide. "Alex, give me a boost."

With Alex shoving, she managed to

scramble on top of Buttercup. Straddling the cow's broad back, she put out her hand. Alex handed her the bundle, which was the blanket from the schoolhouse. Alex hauled himself up and sat behind Mattie. Buttercup shifted her bony hips, but didn't seem to mind the kids on her back. Sophie gave Ellsworth to Mattie, grabbed hold of Alex's wrist, and let him pull her up. She sat behind him on Buttercup's rump.

The thrashing grew louder.

"Hurry," Mattie said. "Get into position before they get here."

Sophie climbed on Alex's shoulders. He gripped her lower legs, while she braced her feet against Mattie's back.

"Here."

Alex took the flashlight from his pocket and handed it to Sophie. She held the flashlight with one hand so it pointed toward her face. Mattie passed Ellsworth up to Sophie, who perched the stuffed elephant on top of her head with her free hand.

Then Mattie unfolded the blanket. Twisting around, she draped it over Sophie, Alex, and herself until they were covered. Only Ellsworth's small head stuck out. Mattie clasped the edges of the blanket loosely so she could see out through the slit.

"Here they come!" she whispered hoarsely.

Gunpowder tore into the clearing. The moon was so bright Mattie could see the horse's eyes rolling in fear. Ichabod Crane clung to his horse's mane. The schoolmaster's knees were up around his shoulders and he looked like a huge cricket.

"Ai-i-e-e-e-e!" he screamed, tossing a glance over his shoulder.

Hard on Gunpowder's heels galloped a gigantic black horse ridden by a black-cloaked headless giant! One upraised arm wielded a sword that gleamed in the moonlight.

Mattie knew the headless horseman was really Brom. The heavy object in the sack swinging from the saddle horn must be the pumpkin. And he was probably peering through the slit in his cloak just as she was.

"Now!" she said.

Sophie switched on the flashlight. As if on cue, Buttercup mooed, low and loud.

Ichabod wheeled Gunpowder in a tight circle and sat upright in the saddle.

"It's us!" Mattie whispered to him. "Don't be scared!"

"You three are a fearsome sight!" Ichabod's voice quavered. "Are you sure the plan you wrote in that note will work?"

"Positive," Mattie said. She was betting that Brom was a big 'fraidy cat, deep inside. At least she hoped he was.

Ichabod seemed to sense her concern. "Don't worry. I'm going to make certain Brom doesn't discover your real identity."

At that moment, the black-cloaked horseman raced toward the bridge. Peering through the slit in the blanket, Mattie saw Daredevil rear up, pawing the mist-filled air.

"AHHHHHHHH!" Brom Bones yelled so loud, Mattie was surprised the water didn't leap out of the stream.

She could imagine what he saw—a great, big strange animal with two humps, a weird body, and a weird little elephant head that was eerily lit. She wished she had a picture of the "new monster" of Sleepy Hollow.

Buttercup mooed again. Daredevil neighed and threw Brom off his back. Teeth clattering like pot lids, Brom scuttled through the woods on his hands and knees. Mattie was sure that his screams could be heard all the way to Virginia. Daredevil galloped off in the opposite direction.

Then she heard something else. Voices— lots of them—on the other side of the woods. Peering through the blanket, Mattie saw dozens of torches bobbing among the trees.

"The villagers are coming," she said to Alex and Sophie. "We need to get out of here before they catch us!"

Gunpowder trotted over. Ichabod slid off Gunpowder's back and looped the reins around a branch.

"Let me assist you," he said, reaching up to help pull off the blanket. "It's the least I can do."

He lifted Sophie down first, and then helped Alex. Mattie tossed Alex the blanket before she slid off the cow.

"Where did Brom go?" asked Sophie.

Ichabod chuckled. "I don't think he'll stop until he's in Canada!"

"Katrina will find out how brave you were tonight," said Mattie. "Will you ask her out?"

Ichabod thought a moment. Then he shook his head. "Since I've discovered I'm not a scaredy-cat, I think I'll see the world. I'm leaving Sleepy Hollow."

The voices and bobbing lights grew closer. Mattie knew they would have to disappear before the villagers arrived.

Ichabod watched Alex slip the flash-light into his pocket. "I know you children aren't witches, but you do possess unearthly powers. Will you show me the magic light stick?"

"I can't," Alex said. He pulled the spyglass from his other pocket.

Mattie nodded. It was time to go.

Just then Katrina rushed into the clearing.

"Ichabod!" she cried. "You're all right!"

"Of course, I am," said Ichabod. "Why wouldn't I be?"

"We saw Brom!" she hurried on. "He was so frightened, he nearly ran us over! We couldn't understand him—something about a mammoth big goblin! Do you know what he was talking about?"

Ichabod held her hand. "There are no goblins," he told her. "No ghosts. And no witches."

Katrina looked at the Mattie, Alex, and Sophie. "I believe you. But I don't know about the rest of the villagers."

"Then let's go talk to them," Ichabod said.

He and Katrina turned and walked toward the crowd that was surging through the trees.

"Now!" Mattie said.

Alex held out the spyglass. Sophie grabbed the middle and Mattie gripped the other end.

Before the familiar tingling spread under her fingertips, Mattie wondered if their vanishing act would become yet another Sleepy Hollow legend.

Then purple, green, and ghost-white swirls sparkled behind her eyelids. Her body twirled through space until—

Thump!

Her feet hit something solid. Mattie opened her eyes. Alex and Sophie stood beside her.

They were back in the tower room. The rain had stopped. Sunlight streamed cheerfully through the long, narrow windows. It was already hot.

"You know," Mattie said. "I don't care how hot it gets. I don't want Halloween in July ever again!"

Alex put the spyglass in its wooden box and placed the box in the desk. "So, Matt, does that mean you believe in ghosts now?"

"I believe there *could* be ghosts and supernatural stuff," she said, opening the front of the desk. She pulled out an envelope. "Let's read the Travel Guide's letter in my room. It's cooler there."

"I wish we could have gone back to the Van Tassels' house before we left Sleepy Hollow," Alex said as he pivoted the secret panel. "They had all that food . . . and I'm hungry."

"You're always hungry," Mattie said, crawling through the opening behind him. She turned. "Soph? What are you doing?"

"Nothing." Sophie stood by the desk. She tugged open a drawer and dropped something brown and crumbly inside.

Mattie sniffed. A sweet, sugary aroma drifted through the air . . . homemade doughnuts?

Dear Mattie, Alex, and Sophie:

I hope you enjoyed your "Halloween in July" trip! Mattie, now that you've opened your mind to ghosts—and other things we can't explain—what else could be possible? Throughout history, people have performed amazing feats because they believed in possibility.

Europeans came to the United States because they thought it was possible to have a better life. Around 1524, Giovanni da Verrazzano, an Italian explorer, sailed near what would later be New York City. He went back to Europe, and others became interested in this new land.

Native Americans already occupied the New World. Two major tribes lived in the area that would later become New York State—the Algonquian and the Iroquois. Other tribes included the Mohawk, Mahican, Seneca, and Oneida. What happened to those tribes—and other groups of Native Americans—is a story for another adventure.

In 1609, Henry Hudson sailed his ship, the Half Moon, up a huge river. Hudson, an Englishman working for the Dutch, reported rich land along this river. Soon Dutch settlers landed in what is now New York City. They moved into the valleys along the Hudson River. They called the area New Netherland and exchanged goods with Native Americans for furs. In those days, furs were like gold.

New Netherland became a British colony in 1664. Although the name was changed to New York, many people still spoke Dutch and kept their Dutch customs, including their superstitions and ghost stories.

People all over the world have their own superstitions. You may have heard that finding a four-leaf clover is good luck. Or that it's bad luck if a black cat crosses your path. Some say owning a black cat brings good luck. Winchester would say so!

Scary stories became popular in England, and later America, when books like Frankenstein and Dracula were published. These books were called Gothic—they often included haunted houses, ghosts, castles, and the supernatural. The most well-known American Gothic writer is Edgar Allan Poe, who wrote "The Raven" and "The Tell-Tale Heart."

The author of "The Legend of Sleepy Hollow," Washington Irving, may have been friends with Poe. Washington Irving was born in New York City in 1783. Later he traveled to Europe, where he read Dutch and German folktales.

In 1820, Irving published a book of stories. Two of the stories, "The Legend of Sleepy Hollow" and "Rip Van Winkle," made him famous. In "The Legend of Sleepy Hollow," Irving borrowed the name Ichabod Crane from an officer he knew during the War of 1812. "Rip Van Winkle" is about man who leaves home to hide in New York's Catskill Mountains. He falls asleep, wakes up twenty years later, and goes back home. Read the story to find out what happened!

After the stories were published, Washington Irving bought a house called Sunnyside in Tarrytown, New York. Sunnyside was the original Van Tassel farmhouse. Irving died in 1859 at the age of seventy-six and was buried in Sleepy Hollow cemetery, near the burying ground of the Old Dutch Church.

Time Spies, your next adventure will make Sophie very happy. That's all I'm allowed to say!

Yours in time,
"Mrs. Sullivan"

TIME SPIES MISSION NO. 6
MAKE SECRET MESSAGE DOUGHNUTS

As spies, you need to be able to send secret messages in unusual places, even at parties. You may not have any special devices for sending messages. Doughnuts can come in handy, as Mattie learned.

Until your next adventure, your mission is to whip up a batch of Secret Message Doughnuts. Just don't eat them all before you send any messages!

WHAT YOU NEED:

A grown-up
Canned biscuit dough
Cooking oil (enough to
float the doughnuts in)
Sugar
Bottle cap from a
2-liter soda bottle

Large pot
Slotted spoon
Paper towels
Resealable plastic bag
Strip of 1 inch wide
paper
Pencil

WHAT YOU DO:

1. Find a grown-up to help you. Ask the grown-up to heat the cooking oil in the pot.

2. Open the biscuit can and pull apart the slices. Make a hole in each biscuit with the bottle cap.

3. Have a grown-up drop the doughnuts into the oil and cook until they are golden brown on both sides. Remove with a slotted spoon and cool on towels.

4. Put the sugar in the plastic bag.

5. Add a cool doughnut and shake well.

6. Write your message on a small strip of paper and roll it up tight.

7. Carefully poke the paper into one of the doughnut holes, like a fortune cookie.

TIME SPIES

"A time-traveling mystery . . . that will keep kids turning the pages!"
—Marcia T. Jones,
co-author of *The Bailey School Kids*

Give an important message to General Washington in
Secret in the Tower

Catch a dinosaur thief in
Bones in the Badlands

Climb into the pages of *Jack and the Beanstalk* in
Giant in the Garden

Help legendary magician Harry Houdini in
Magician in the Trunk

Reunite a Civil War spy with his brother in
Signals in the Sky

Unmask the Headless Horseman in
Rider in the Night
AUGUST 2007

Save the Race of the Century in
Horses in the Wind
NOVEMBER 2007

For more information visit:
www.timespies.com